DAVID'S MIGHTIEST
Warriors

LAVOYN JONES

To order additional copies of this book, contact:
Bookwhip
1-855-339-3589
https://www.bookwhip.com

There were thirty-seven Mighty Men according to the book of Deuteronomy. They were all superior fighters and acted as King David's special Forces. They were completely loyal and devoted to their king. Though they fought and won many battles for King David, there is little mention of them in the Bible beyond their name and the name of the towns where they were born. Three, were set apart from the others by having their greatest battles mentioned in the Bible. Here are their stories.

"What are you doing Shammah?" asked Eleazar.

"Oh, just being a good soldier. Sit down and I'll show you the proper way to sharpen a sword."

"And how could you show me such a thing when you sit there rubbing your sword with the stone? Everyone knows that you are supposed to hold the stone still and stroke it with the sword."

"That would not be wise." Shammah said seriously. "You could actually dull your sword that way."

"Really?" asked Eleazar. "Why don't we ask Adino."

"Very well, let us ask him."

Adino was nearby practicing with his spear. "Adino!" Eleazar called. "Come here for a moment would you?" Adino stopped what he was doing and cradling his spear in his right arm like a sleeping baby, walked over to where his two friends were seated.

"What are you two arguing about this time?"

"It's a matter of weapons maintenance." Said Eleazar.

Just then a soldier approached the three friends fire. "David has announced that we will be attacking a Philistine company which will be passing through this area just a little south of here."

"Then we had best get our rest instead of bickering over the best way to sharpen weapons," said Shammah.

"Agreed," said Eleazar. "With enough rest Shammah should be able to beat our enemies to death with his dull sword."

"Thank you, for that confidence my friend. I pray that the Lord grants you, equal strength," replied Shammah. "Ha ha ha," laughed Eleazar. "Amen, my brother, amen."

The next day David had his men wait in a bowl shaped valley in a field of lentil while he and his captains climbed the ridge, so as to look down on the approaching Philistines. When they topped a distant rise David and his men were unpleasantly surprised.

"There are more of them than our scouts reported yesterday," said David. "Another company must have joined them this morning."

"Yes, almost ten times our number," said one of the captains. "Perhaps three hundred in all."

"Quickly," said David. "Get our men out of that valley and back up into the hills before they are surrounded and slaughtered."

Shammah

There he is, the boy I was telling you about," said a young man to his friend. They watched from behind a tree as a boy, pulled a piece of wood out of a small damn allowing water from a stream to fill a small pond from which the goat heard could drink.

"You can't be serious," said the friend. "That, little boy defeated Master Aegee in unarmed combat?"

"Its true, I was there. That's Shammah, Master Aegee's son. The Master has been teaching him everything he knows from the day that he took his first step."

"But, he looks to be the same size as my cousin Eili. How old is he, nine?"

"No, he is small for his age. He is actually twelve."

"Still, it's hard to believe…"

"Why are you two standing here talking?" said a familiar voice from behind the two friends. "You haven't finished with your exercises that quickly have you?"

"No, Master Aegee," they said in unison as they turned to face their combat skills instructor. "We'll get started on them right away sir," said the first young man.

"Since you seem to have so much time on your hands, you can do every exercise twice."

The first young man half opened his mouth as if he were about to protest. Then quickly changed his mind, remembering from past experience that arguing would only make the Master angry. He simply answered. "Yes, Master Aegee."

When he saw that his father had returned Shammah ran to greet him. But he knew better than to interrupt when his father was addressing his students. He waited until his father turned from the students.

"Father, mother has set out everything for our trip to uncle Kademius' house. We can go when you're ready."

Agee set two of the older students in charge and said good bye to his wife before he and Shammah left. Their trip lasted for three days and was uneventful. On the fourth morning they started the long walk home. "Uncle Kademius has a really nice house. We should add another floor to our house." Said Shammah.

Aegee chuckled as he walked. "And what would we do with this second floor? Your uncle has six children, there are only three of us."

"I was thinking you could use it for training your students when the weather is bad."

Just then three men stepped out from behind some trees growing at the roadside. They were dirty, their clothes were old and worn and the swords they carried looked like they had been used to break rocks, then resharpened.

"Give us your money and we'll let you live." Said the one with a scar across his forehead. "You men are making a mistake," said Aegee. "You've picked the wrong people to rob today."

"Just shut up and toss us your money bag." Said the skinny one.

"Father," said Shammah. "May I handle this?"

"Are you sure my son? You will have to kill them you know." Shammah took a deep breath. "I know father."

"Ha ha, did you hear that?" said the third bandit, who happened to have a surprisingly deep voice. "He's going to send his little boy against us."

"Hey boy, why does your father hate you so much that he would rather see you die than give up his money?" asked the skinny one.

Shammah drew his sword and slowly advanced on the trio.

"Don't do this boy," said the one with the scar. "We won't hesitate to kill you. We've killed children before."

"Then you are murderers as well as thieves, you deserve death." Said Shammah.

Then he attacked them. He faked a high arcing swing at the deep voiced one's head. Causing him to raise his sword to block the attack. Only to have Shammah change the direction of his sword mid way through the swing. He brought his sword down, took a quick step to the right, and then up through the deep voiced man's ribs and into his heart just under his left armpit. Shammah quickly withdrew his sword and pivoted on his left foot, then slashed the throat of the stunned and unmoving skinny man with a sudden backhand motion. He let his sword continue down and around and made an upward slash at the scarred man. But his attack was blocked. His arm continued up over his head and came down in a slashing attack aimed at the scarred man's chest. This too was blocked. Then the thief raised his sword in what would surely have been a skull-splitting blow. But Shammah's recovery was too quick for him. He stopped with his sword still over his head and looked down to find the boy's sword deep in his stomach. Shammah pulled his sword free as the man fell. With his enemy's blood dripping from his sword he surveyed his handy work. He had heard stories about men who got sick or shook uncontrollably after their first kill but neither of these was his reaction. He was excited, thrilled. He was disappointed that there had not been more of them.

Aegee was proud of his son's skill, until he saw his eyes. Then, he began to worry, his son's eyes were those of someone who enjoyed killing.

Shammah did enjoy killing. But he had no interest in indiscriminate mayhem. He wanted to kill Philistines.

They were far worst than the thieves he and his father had encountered on the road. They not only stole but also, raped murdered and sometimes even tortured people for no reason. They were a plague on the land, is what his father had once told him. That was why the town elders had asked him to teach their sons to fight, so that if they were ever attacked they would not fall like slaughtered sheep.

The encounter with the three thieves proved to Shammah that he was ready to start making a difference. He might not be able to kill all of the Philistines in Israel. But, by doing what he could, perhaps one less woman would be abused, one less child would be maimed, one less man of Israel would be murdered. He was ready, ready to go hunting for Philistines.

Three days after their return from Kademius' house Shammah went to Aegee and asked if he could go hunting.

"Shammah, the Philistine scouts and patrols are being seen these days more often than ever before in the hills to the north. Many have seen them and have grown concerned. Therefore they have sent their sons to me, that I may teach them the use of the sword. I now have twice as many students as I had before our trip."

"Father, I can hunt on my own. You have taught me well and we are running low on dried meat. What will we feed the new students?"

Aegee's eyes narrowed as he thought for a moment. Shammah had never shown a great enthusiasm for hunting when he had taken him in the past. So why did he suddenly want to go hunting, even if it meant going alone?

Aegee's eyes narrowed further with that thought. Perhaps going alone was exactly what he desired. Perhaps he was looking for a way to satisfy his newly found desire for killing. "Very well," said Aegee. "You may go hunting. Just be sure to avoid the Philistine patrols."

Shammah smiled broadly. "Yes Father, thank you Father." He left quickly to go and prepare for his hunting trip. Aegee sighed and prayed. "Mighty God, protect my son and guide him as only you can. Amen."

The next day Shammah was in the foothills above his village. He was sweating because of the late afternoon sun and stiff from crouching behind a boulder for hours. He watched the road. It wasn't the main road. That would have been too dangerous. It had actually started as an animal trail; it was not called a road until men found that it was more convenient than the main road. Though, not wide enough for a patrol, a scout or messenger would not pass up this shorter and more convenient route.

But no one came up the road all day. The sun was getting low on the horizon and Shammah was considering leaving his position when he heard voices echoing off the rocks. Then around the bend came two Philistine scouts. Shammah quietly drew his sword. The road would bring them right past his position. As soon as they stepped past his boulder, Shammah thrust his sword into the neck of the man closest to him, severing the artery and releasing a fountain of blood.

The second man had not seen Shammah; just the spurting blood and his comrades strangled cry. As the wounded man fell, Shammah was revealed. The Philistine quickly reached for his sword. But with a flick of his wrist, Shammah threw the blood dripping from his sword into the solder's eyes. He backed away as he frantically used both hands to clear his vision. But it was no use. Shammah ran to him and plunged his sword deep into the soldier's breast, piercing his heart. Remembering his father's training, he quickly snatched his sword free and turned to look at the wounded man.

He was getting back to his feet, with one hand on his still bleeding neck and the other holding his sword, using it as a support to raise himself into a standing position.

Shammah allowed him to stand, then beckoned him to attack. The Philistine did not hesitate; he came at Shammah growling. But Shammah easily defended himself against the weakened soldier's attack and with a powerful backhanded stroke, slashed the soldier's neck, removing one of his fingers in the process.

Shammah hid the bodies in a space between two large rocks. Then piled more rocks in the opening to keep any animals from dragging them out. The Philistines would have no idea what became of their scouts.

On the way home he happened upon a grazing gazelle and realized that he had forgotten that he was supposed to be hunting. He gave thanks to God and quickly reached for his bow and killed it with one arrow. Shammah continued in this manner for three years. Then one day while he watched the sheep and no one else was near by, one of his father's older students came and spoke with him.

"Shammah, my name is Elishammah."

"God be with you." Said Shammah.

"And also with you, and I truly believe that he is with you since you are still alive."

"What do you mean by that?" asked Shammah.

"Just that I enjoy hunting also and that I noticed that you always come back with a kill. So I decided to follow you one day with the intention of learning your hunting secrets. I was very surprised to find you lying in wait next to a road. I was even more surprised to see you ambush three Philistines."

"You must be very good, I had no idea that I was being watched."

"Your father says that my skills at tracking and spying are superior to any he has trained before."

"I see, and why are you talking to me and not reporting my deeds to my father?"

"He would make you stop. But I would like to join you. There are also two others who are very skilled and would like an opportunity to kill Philistines."

Shammah looked into the young man's eyes and could see a fierce determination there. He pondered the idea. If he turned Elishammah down, he might tell Shammah's father what he had seen. Though, more likely he and his friends would simply start going out on hunting trips of their own.

On the other hand, the addition of three men to his efforts would help rid the land of the Philistine plague that much sooner.

"Very well," said Shammah. "I will tell my father that I have found some friends to go hunting with next week. He never liked it when I went out alone, so this news will please him."

A week later Shammah led his new friends Elishammah, Ira and Gareb to a mountain road on which he had seen several Philistine patrols. They traveled south on the road until they came to a place where it was bordered by a steep hill on one side with large rocks near the top of the hill that they could hide behind.

Because he knew that none of the others had ever killed anyone before, Shammah planned to make it as easy on them as possible. "We'll hide behind those rocks up there and wait for a small patrol. When they get to this spot I'll give the signal and we will take them with arrows."

The others liked his plan and they were soon in position waiting for a patrol.

It did not take long, twenty minutes later; Elishammah gave a soft whistle and pointed north. Five Philistines were coming down the road, one in front, the others following two by two.

On Shammah's signal they all stood and fired. Four arrows were shot and four Philistines fell. But two quickly got up and ran for cover. One had been struck in the left arm and the other in the right leg. The fifth man aided the latter.

By the time Shammah, who was the quickest, had knocked his second arrow the two slower men had almost reached cover. The one with the arrow in his arm managed to reach cover and was readying his bow, to return fire.

Shammah aimed at the back of the uninjured man, only to have the one with an arrow in his leg stumble, causing his helper to turn an instant before the arrow hit him. So instead of being killed he was only wounded as the arrow entered through his back and stopped with the point sticking out from under his right arm. Shammah noticed that the others had missed the quickly moving target. He reached down for his third arrow and stopped. He caught a distant movement out of the corner of his eye; he turned his head to see what it might be. He gasped when he recognized another patrol, this one had ten men they had seen the fighting and were running to help their comrades.

Shammah called to the others, "There's another patrol coming, Elishammah come with me. You two stay and finish here."

Shammah slung his quiver over his shoulder and took off running over the top of the ridge toward the approaching patrol. Elishammah quickly snatched up his own quiver and followed.

At some time in the past two boulders that had at one time been on the hill, came loose and rolled down it, stopping in the brush on the opposite side of the road. The wounded Philistines were now hiding behind those boulders. One was bigger than a man was and the other was almost chest high. The archer, the one with the arrow in his arm was behind the smaller boulder. He stood and fired over the boulder at the snipers. But his arrow fell short. He was obviously having trouble holding his bow with an arrow in his arm.

Ira turned to Gareb and said, "I'll take the archer, you take the other two." Gareb agreed and began to study the situation.

Ira noticed that the rocks that Shammah and Elishammah had been hiding behind continued for quite a distance.

If he could get over to them without being seen he could fire on the archer from a new angle. So he got on his belly with bow and quiver in hand, and started to crawl.

Gareb saw that there was a split in the rock behind which the two Philistines were hiding. The one with an arrow in his leg kept peeking around the side of the rock, and every time he would duck back behind it Gareb could see the back of his head through the crack. Gareb calmed himself and took careful aim. He knew he had to do this on the first attempt, because if they realized where he was aiming they would be sure to avoid the opening. There was a light breeze blowing in his face so he aimed a little high and released, at the same moment the Philistine peeked around the rock and snatched his head back as soon as he saw the arrow. The arrow passed through the crack and into his head.

Ira reached his new position and took a quick look over the rocks, there was the archer, he could see him from the side. And though he could hit the man, the angle did not promise a sure kill. Just then Gareb fired an arrow; it appeared to pass through the top of the larger boulder. But the sound was not the sound of an arrow striking stone; neither did it sound like flesh being struck. The archer looked to his left then yelled a curse at Gareb. He reached for an arrow. Ira knew he was about to get his chance at a kill shot, so he quickly readied his bow. The archer stood, aiming toward Gareb, but his shot didn't even come close to the target because Ira's arrow had pierced the base of his neck, causing a fountain of blood to spray the rock in front of him. Seeing this caused Ira to vomit unexpectedly.

Gareb knew where the second man had to be there was only so much room behind that rock. And with an arrow in his back it was doubtful that he would be doing a lot of moving around. It was easy to tell that the Philistine was still alive. He was shouting a steady stream of insults and curses at Gareb. And challenging him to come down and fight hand to hand. Since the archers were dead Gareb stood up to assess the situation. Though he had heard them die he could not see their bodies. As he stood there listening to the breeze and the sound of Ira retching far off to his left. The words of Aegee came to mind. He had once said, "Never assume an enemy is dead until you have thrust your sword into him."

The soldier may not be as badly injured as they thought. Accepting his challenge and going down to fight him face to face may be some kind of trap.

"So how do you shoot an arrow into an enemy who is hidden and will not show himself?" Gareb thought, "I need to do this quickly, Elishammah and Shammah may need help."

Because the large rocks along the way hid them the men on the road did not see the two young warriors running along the ridge. Shammah was racing for the relatively clear slope he had seen earlier. When he reached it he made a sharp turn and without slowing his pace ran down the steep hill continuously firing arrows as he went. Elishammah could not believe that they were doing this, but he did not hesitate. He followed Shammah's daredevil lead and fired his own arrows as he went, praying to God for surefootedness and accuracy.

Shammah remembered the training exercise his father had given him; it had seemed foolish at the time. He had been told to run back and forth while trying to shoot a swinging target. He had quickly mastered the task, but he had to admit that it had taught him to run with as little bounce as possible and how to watch where he was going while at the same time not losing sight of his target. But that had been on level ground, and an even surface. He was now running down a rough and very steep hill. He aimed for the center of the last man's chest and pierced his left eye. He tried for the same spot on the next man and struck him in the lower stomach. The third would have been struck in the chest except Shammah slipped slightly on some loose gravel. His arrow found the man's throat instead. Just as he reached the road his fourth arrow hit it's intended mark striking the Philistine in the heart.

Elishammah had similar trouble with his aim, striking one man in the forehead, one in the groin and a third in the leg.

Shammah dropped his bow and pulled his sword from his belt. The man with the arrow in his leg managed to parry the first two thrusts, but fell before Shammah's merciless onslaught.

Elishammah, upon reaching the road also threw aside his bow, drew his sword and cut the throat of the man with the arrow in his groin. The remaining four men had split up. Two had gone behind a pile of boulders on the left side of the road and the other two had gone behind the even larger boulders on the right.

The breeze picked up a little as he looked down on the enemies hiding place, pushing his hair back slightly. This gave Gareb an idea. He shot an arrow high into the air and in the direction of the boulder. The wind caught it as it came down and caused it to land in the road. He adjusted his aim and shot another arrow high into the air. This one landed just in front of the rock. Gareb adjusted his aim again, this time the arrow landed behind the rock. But the sound it made was not from striking dirt or stone but that of an arrow striking flesh. A moment later an arm flopped out from behind the boulder as if someone in a sitting position had fallen to the side with their arm stretched out, the Philistine was dead.

Gareb noticed then that his hands had started to shake. And try as he might, he could not stop them.

Shammah went after the two on the right. And Elishammah went after the other two, on the opposite side of the road.

Shammah slowly moved into what turned out to be a maze, made up of boulders and rock piles. He could hear the occasional loose rock rattle against others as his enemies fled before him. He knew that they would try to ambush him, and quickly, since the maze could not be very large given the size of the hill it's rocks had fallen from. He turned sideways to get through a narrow spot, then stopped. He had seen a sword tip disappear behind the boulder he was about to squeeze past. He brought his sword up into a defensive position and as he did so he heard a small amount of gravel fall just ahead of him and to the left. It was directly across from the hidden man. Shammah could not see any place to hide in that direction except if one were to climb on top of the rocks and perhaps leap upon the enemy while he was distracted by your comrade in arms. Shammah took a moment to determine what the perfect positioning might be then continued forward. He leapt past the hidden man, instead of merely stepping out past the end of the rock. Just as Shammah had hoped, the Philistine had not expected him to move that quickly. He brought his sword down on nothing with all his might, throwing himself off balance. Shammah stabbed him in the side, puncturing his lung; there was a shuffling sound above and behind him. Shammah snatched his sword free and skewered the second man in midair as he leapt down from his hiding place.

Elishammah carefully entered the jumble of chest high rocks, but he only took three steps before he was attacked. The Philistine must have miscalculated his attack. When he jumped out from his hiding place he was so close to Elishammah that they nearly bumped heads. Elishammah grabbed the attackers raised sword arm with his left hand and brought up his own sword. But the Philistine grabbed his sword arm as well. As they wrestled back and forth Elishammah tripped over a rock and momentarily lost his balance. It was all the Philistine needed to drive him back against a rock and slam his head on it, the intense pain caused him to drop his sword. But losing his weapon only caused Elishammah to fight harder. Then he remembered his unarmed combat training. He saw master Aegee standing before the class reminding them to use their enemies' strength against them.

"Alright, that is what I must do." Elishammah thought to himself, "My enemy is bigger, stronger, and has me against a rock."

Suddenly Elishammah had an idea and before it was even formed in his own mind, he acted. He dropped to his knees and pulled his arms down with all his might. Since the Philistine had been pushing against him as hard as he could the sudden maneuver caused him to practically leap headfirst into the rock he had been pressing Elishammah against. Elishammah smiled at the crunching noise the soldier's head made as it slammed against the stone. But the smile quickly disappeared as the second soldier came screaming from behind some rocks. Running with his sword raised above his head. Elishammah shoved the first soldier's lifeless body into the second soldier's path. He easily dogged it but in doing so he was forced to move away from Elishammah. It delayed him but a moment. But that was more than enough time for Elishammah to retrieve his sword. The second soldier bounded toward him determined to split Elishammah's skull before he regained his feet.

The moment his hand touched his sword Elishammah had rolled over into a sitting position. The Philistine was nearly upon him and he could think of only one way to attack. He kicked the rock, with the first soldier's blood still trailing down it's face, and spun himself around, leaned back and stabbed the second soldier in the stomach just as he started to bring down his sword on the place that only a fraction of a second earlier had contained Elishammah's head. Elishammah snatched his sword free and quickly rolled to his left so that the Philistine would not fall on him. This brought him face to face with the blank lifeless stare and bloody caved in forehead of the first soldier. He held the gaze of those soulless orbs for only a moment, then turned away, barley avoiding the shame of having his vomit spew forth into the dead mans face.

After completely emptying his stomach and a few dry heaves, Elishammah looked up to find Shammah watching him. Shammah offered his hand and helped him to his feet. Elishammah noticed that his hands had started to shake like wind blown leaves. He also noticed that Shammah never mentioned it.

"What have you been doing?" Asked Aegee, when Shammah entered the house with an armload of animal skins.

"What do you mean father? I told you I was going hunting with my friends," said Shammah.

"Yes, that is what you told me. But since when does it take two weeks to hunt anything. And I know your hunting skills, because I am the very one who taught them to you. Am I so poor a teacher that you return with only one, two, three skins?"

"The hunt did not go well." Shammah replied as he flopped onto a large cushion.

"Your hunting has not gone well the last three times you have gone out. I suspect the truth has something to do with the small army of Philistines that came here looking for a band of Israelite warriors who have been attacking their patrols."

Shammah suddenly pushed himself up into an alert position. "Was any one hurt?" he quickly asked.

"No," said Aegee. "No one was harmed, but they could have been. If you wish to fight the Philistines so badly, then do it the right way. Go to Jerusalem and join King Saul's army. At least that way you will not place the people you love in danger.

"Yes, I will. I'll leave tomorrow. I' m sorry father."

"Do not be sorry, I knew this day was coming."

Shammah left the next day with friends, the same three that had gone raiding with him. After two days the young men came to the town of Ramah. As they approached the town a boy who was sitting on a stone on the side of the road called out to them. "Are one of you Shammah, son of Aegee?"

"Yes, I am." Said Shammah. "How do you know my name, I have never been here before."

"My master Samuel, the Prophet, sent me to watch for you. He said the Lord has a message for you. But you must hurry for he is very old and in bed with an illness, he may not recover."

"Then take us to him quickly" said Shammah.

The whole group ran behind the boy to Samuel's home. But only Shammah was allowed to enter.

The old prophet's room was well lit. Even though the noonday sun brightened the room it was still cool and comfortable.

Samuel was sitting up in bed, with several pillows propping him up. But to Shammah he appeared to be asleep, until he spoke.

"Come in Shammah, son of Aegee." His voice was weak so Shammah sat close to him, so that he would not miss anything that was said to him.

"The Lord says that it is good that you wish to fight the Philistines. But Saul will soon be dead. David will be the new king. Serve me, by serving him. Thus sayeth the Lord."

"But David is in hiding. Does he know that Saul is to die soon, and how will I find him?"

Samuel held up his hand to silence the young man. "Pass through Jerusalem and continue down to Hebron. You will meet David there."

"Thank you great prophet. My men and I shall leave this very day."

"No no," said Samuel. "There is no need to rush. David will not arrive in Hebron until twenty days from now.

Spend the night here, rest, and eat. Then, in the morning you can continue your journey."

Shammah agreed. The next morning he and his men set out for Jerusalem. They stayed there for seven days so that they could purchase animals and make sin and fellowship offerings.

While there they heard about a great battle, and Saul's death. They also heard that David was grieving for Saul. "It takes a special kind of man to grieve for someone who wanted to kill you," said Elishammah.

Shammah replied, "Perhaps that is why the Lord chose him to be King of Israel."

As David's men began their retreat Shammah turned to his friends. "I will remain here, hidden in the lentils, and make sure that none of their scouts report our position."

"Then we will see you in camp." said Adino.

He and Eleazar both knew that Shammah was an excellent warrior and very capable when it came to ambushing a few scouts. They left, confident that their friend could take care of himself.

Less than an hour later Shammah felt the spirit of the Lord come upon him. He was filled with strength and a confidence that was not his own. Something deep inside of him said. "There is no need to hide, stand, that I might deliver your enemies into you hand."

So Shammah stood and faced the ridge. A moment later the Philistine company crested the ridge and saw the lone warrior standing in the field.

"Any of you who come into this field will die today." Shammah yelled loud enough for all of them to hear. "Sir, shall I call forth the archers so that this fool can be killed quickly?" the Philistine Captain asked his Commander.

"No," said the Commander. "Send two men against him armed with swords. I wish to see the skill that makes one believe he can stand against three hundred."

The two Philistines came at Shammah with the caution of seasoned veterans. But they had barley raised their swords against him before his sword found their hearts.

"The Lord has greatly increased my strength and speed." thought Shammah, to himself. "Its as if they were standing there, waiting for me to strike."

The Lord also touched the mind of the Philistine Commander, multiplying his pride and his anger, and removing his reason. So that he sent wave after wave of his soldiers against Shammah. First in twos then in groups of four then in groups of eight, and finally in groups of twenty. But it was always the same. His men could not touch Shammah and most of them died before they could swing their swords three times.

Finally, all that was left were the Commander and his three Captains. And even though Shammah was now breathing heavily from exhaustion, one of the Captains said to the Commander. "This man fights like a god. We can not defeat him."

The Commander turned to him, enraged. Drew his sword and struck the captain in the neck, nearly removing his head. Then he said to the remaining Captains. "Should we return home and be known as the men who ran from a single Israelite? I think it would be better to die hear with our men."

The Captains agreed with their Commander's reasoning and they all attacked as one. Shammah killed them as easily as the others.

Adino and Eleazar had began to worry about their friend. He had been gone far to long and they were concerned that something may have happened to him. So they went to David and told him that they were going to look for their friend. David decided to go with them along with a few others. They arrived at the lentil field only a few moments after Shammah had finished with the Commander and his two Captains. They found him standing unsteadily in the middle of a field covered with dead men.

"What happened here?" David asked when he reached Shammah.

Shammah answered, "The Lord spoke to me and said, "Stand before your enemies and I will deliver them into your hand. So I stood."

Eleazar

"What is this Tamuz?" Eleazar asked his little sister as he snatched the object from her hand. "Give it back, Eleazar!"

"I will, in a minute." The object which had held his sisters attention so intently that he was able to walk right up to her and watch her play with it for a few seconds, was a new doll. "Mother must have made it for her," he surmised. It was a simple thing, made of cloth and from the feel of it, stuffed with the leavings of other sewing projects. Eleazar had trouble getting a good look at it though because he had to keep turning this way and that in order to keep Tamuz from grabbing it as she continually demanded the return of her new toy. Eleazar added to her frustration by laughing at her every time she grabbed for the doll and missed. He even started holding it over her head just low enough so that it was almost in reach, then lifting it higher when she would jump for it. She new it was of no use to try, but she tried any way. It didn't help that her brother was tall for a thirteen-year-old. He was almost as tall as their father, whom every one considered to be a tall man.

Tamuz had quickly grown tired of her brother's game. Her mood suddenly changed from frustration to anger. She released that anger by kicking her brother in the shin. Eleazar dropped the doll and hopped on his good leg while rubbing the injured one. Tamuz quickly retrieved her doll, but as she straightened up from picking up her toy he pushed her, causing her to land hard on her bottom. And just in time for his mother to see him place his hand on Tamuz's head and shove, as she entered the house.

"Eleazar, why must you torment your sister?"

Before he could answer Tamuz blurted out everything that had happened, in one long almost incomprehensible sentence. Leaving out, of course, the fact that she had kicked him. Then, just to be sure his fate was sealed, she burst into a staggered breathing, body shaking, crying fit. If he hadn't known better, Eleazar could have sworn she was doing it on purpose. But the fact that she wasn't only made him feel bad about himself in addition to making him look bad.

"Your father will not be pleased to hear of this. You should be ashamed of the way you treat her, like a dog."

"Just leave me alone."

Perhaps it was because his shin was still aching, or maybe because he knew that there was nothing he could do to change his mother's mind and keep her from telling his father what she had seen. Whatever the reason was, he regretted those words the moment he had spoken them.

Tamuz's mouth dropped open, astonished by her brother's behavior. She slowly turned her head to see her mother's reaction.

She had a wide-eyed look of surprise on her face and she was holding her breath. She slowly exhaled and as she did her face drew up into an ugly face filled with the fury of a mother pushed too far. "How dare you speak to me that way." She whispered. All thought of waiting until her husband returned flew from her mind. She quickly went to the wall next to the cooking pot and took down a large spoon. Which happened to be a duel purpose tool. Most of the time it was for cooking, but sometimes it was for correction. Her son was in need of correction. She turned to face him, but he was gone. She hated it when he did that, while at the same time admiring such quite, quickness in someone so large.

When Dodai, Eleazar's father, heard of his sons behavior he went to his son and punished him with a wooden rod and much work.

A few days later Dodai was in town speaking with a new client about a stone work project when a familiar voice called out to him from behind.

"Dodai, is that you?"

Dodai turned around and laughed out loud when he saw who had called him. It was Akell. He was Dodai's father's cousin and had been the leader of the fighting men in Dodai's village when he was growing up. Dodai was a little surprised to see how old he looked. But what should he have expected. Akell had been a grown man when he was just a boy.

Dodai hugged the old man and kissed his face before remembering that Akell never cared for that sort of thing. The hug he gave in return was more of a one armed pat on the back and he made no attempt to kiss his second cousin.

Dodai asked Akell to wait while he quickly concluded his business, then took him to an inn where they reminisced about old times and got caught up on each others lives since they had last spoken, almost ten years earlier.

"You have not mentioned your son," said Dodai, after they had spoken for some time.

"Yes, you remember the terrible time when sickness passed through the land? My wife and two of my sons died from it. But my oldest son was strong enough to fight off the disease."

"I thank God for that, what has become of him?

Akell's face became angry and hard. "He and his family were killed by raiders who wanted to steal his goats, about two years ago."

"I'm sorry Akell, I did not mean to upset you. I didn't know."

"It's alright. What of your family? I seem to recall a boy, barely out of diapers."

"That would be Eleazar. I also have a daughter now as well."

"And she is just as beautiful as I remember her mother being, isn't she?"

"What can a proud father say except for, yes. And when she comes of age there is likely to be no end to the line of suitors for my daughters hand."

"Ha ha, she must be beautiful indeed. And your son? What type of man is he growing up to be?"

"I wish that I could say something good. But actually he worries me."

"What do you mean?"

"Well, he is big for his age and very confident in himself. He often bullies his little sister and other children. He has even started to speak rudely to his mother. I believe that one day he will even lose respect for me, and speak rudely to my face. If that should happen I am not sure I would be able to control my self."

"I am very sad to hear this, my friend. But I believe that I may be able to help you. Many boys with the very same attitude as your son have been helped by instruction in military discipline."

"I don't think I would like that. I want my son to be a mason, like me and my father before me. I have been teaching him the craft and there is much more for him to learn."

"But without proper discipline, will the boy do well?'

Dodai sighed and shook his head. "I don't know," he admitted. "But I do know that military training is not something I want for him. He is my only son."

"I understand. If you change your mind come and see me. I have a small place on the east side of town. Just ask anyone, they will be able to tell you how to find old Akell's house."

Dodai clapped him on the shoulder. "Thank you cousin, I must be going now. I have much work to do for this new customer. I will pay you a visit sometime soon."

"Bring the family with you. I would like to see them all."

Dodai returned home and was not pleased to hear the familiar sound of his wife yelling at their son. Dodai went to the window to watch and listen.

"What were you thinking, fighting that boy. He never did anything to you. You knocked him unconscious, you could have killed him."

"I don't think I could have killed him mother. Besides, he's older and bigger than I am. And don't forget I was knocked unconscious as well."

Dodai could only see Eleazar from behind but he did seem to be favoring his left leg, his cloths were dirty and torn and he was holding a moist cloth against his right eye.

"Why do you do these things?" his mother cried. "You are becoming an evil person and I won't have it. I'll beat the evil out of you if I have to." She started smacking him on the head, standing on her toes to reach that high. She also smacked his face over and over again.

Eleazar managed to block most of the blows. But then she made solid contact with his sore eye. No one else noticed, but he certainly felt it. He lashed out blindly, shoving his mother away. She stumbled backward against the fire pit and the hem of her robe was set ablaze.

To Dodai it looked as if the boy had calmly shoved his mother into the fire. Tamuz came running with a blanket, Dodai had not even realized that she was in the room, and wrapped it around her mother's legs, instantly extinguishing the flames. Dodai had seen enough; he went around to the door.

"Mother!" said Eleazar as the pain in his eye subsided and he looked up to see Tamuz putting out her burning robe. He took a step toward her and just then the most heart breaking thing he had ever seen occurred. Both his mother and sister cringed in fear of him.

The front door burst open and Dodai stormed in. "Don't speak, Eleazar. I saw everything from the window. Come with me," he grabbed Eleazar's tunic with his powerful stone cutters hand and nearly yanked him off his feet as he left the house.

Even though he was limping Eleazar trotted to keep up with his fathers quick pace. He knew he had better keep up or he would be dragged through the dirt.

Nearly two hours later they arrived at Akell's house. Eleazar was left standing outside while his father went in to speak with the old man who had answered the door.

A short time later they came out. "Eleazar, this is your cousin Akell. You will be living with him for a while. He has much to teach you. The more quickly you learn, the sooner you will be able to come home. But you may not come home, until he says you are ready to do so."

"Yes, father." Eleazar knew better than to protest, besides this did not seem nearly as bad as one of his father's beatings.

After Dodai had thanked his cousin and left Eleazar started to go into the house so that he could sit down and get off of his sore leg.

Where are you going?" snapped Akell in a voice tinged with disgust. "In the house. I need to rest my sore leg."

"You don't have time for rest, you have work to do. I want you to water the goats, clean the camel stalls, brush the horses, cut fire wood and cook the evening meal."

"The evening meal? It's not even mid day yet. What about the mid day meal?"

"Did you prepare a mid day meal?"

"Of course not. I just got here."

"Well I only made enough for one, so you will have to do without until the evening meal."

"Look Akell…"

"You will refer to me as Master Akell or just Master," Akell shouted.

"Yes, Master Akell," Eleazar said, a little surprised at the old mans change in manner. "As I was about to say. I'm tired and bruised; I have an injured leg and an injured eye. I need to lye down for a while.

"You nearly burned your mother to death, and you are actually going to stand there and tell me about a few bruises and think that I will care? You should thank All Mighty God that I do not simply beat you to death with my staff. Now get to work!"

A week later Eleazar approached Akell. He was mending a broken shutter. "Master, my father said that I was here to learn. But I've been here a week and you have not taught me anything."

"You have just learned your first lesson. If you don't know something, ask a question. Only God knows what a person is thinking. We, are only men, therefore we must talk to one another."

"I spent a week working from sun up to sun down because you were waiting for me to ask a question?" Eleazar asked angrily.

"It worked, did it not? You did ask a question."

"I'm leaving."

"And where will you go? Your father will not let you back into his house until I say you are ready to return." Eleazar took a deep breath, to calm himself. He had been taking a lot of deep breaths for the past week. He did not realize that this was also a lesson, that Akell wanted him to learn self-control.

"To answer your question," Akell continued. "I am to teach you how to be a good fighting man."

"You're going to teach me how to use a sword?"

"There is more to being a fighting man, than using a sword. First of all you are to weak."

"Weak? I'm, the second largest boy in town and there are only two that I know of who are stronger than I am."

"Do not compare yourself to others, they are also weak. When I am done with you, you will think back to this day and say yes, I was weak."

"Alright, Master Akell, when do I start?"

"You already have. The work I am having you do is making you stronger. But you are doing it to slowly. For now on I want you to finish everything as quickly as you can and we will use the remaining daylight to work on sword training. Also I want you to spend a portion of each day removing the rocks from that field over there so that I may plant some vegetables."

"Won't I be to tired at the end of the day for sword training?"

"When you are not tired at the end of the day, then you will know that you are strong."

"That's impossible."

"Not if you pray and ask God to give you strength."

Eleazar did as he was instructed. After the first day of doing all of his work as fast as he could there was still an hour of daylight left. But he was so exhausted that he could hardly stand upright. Picking up a practice sword was completely out of the question. The next day Eleazar prayed that the Lord would strengthen him, but he did not finish his work until after dark. He was so sore and stiff from the day before that he moved slower instead of faster.

"Master Akell, how can I get all of my work done when I am so stiff and sore that I can hardly move?"

"That is the enemy speaking to you, the banished angel. He would have you believe that this is to hard, when in fact you have almost past threw the hardest portion of your journey. If you stay true and do not turn from the task you have set fore yourself God will reward you, not only with strength but endurance. Endurance of the body and of the heart."

"Then I will not listen to what the evil one has to say. I will continue until God strengthens me."

After six months of hard work, Eleazar was ready to return home. He was two inches taller and even though he had been a large young man to begin with his muscles were much larger now. They looked and were, harder and more defined. He had also learned many important things from Akell about being a man, thinking things through, and treating others the way you would want to be treated. All, things that his father had tried to teach him but he had refused to listen to. He even had a new and useful skill. Akell had taught him a sword fighting technique that capitalized on his size and strength while at the same time allowing him to be surprisingly fast.

Unfortunately, what should have been a very happy time for Eleazar turned into a bittersweet one. The day before Eleazar was to be taken home and presented to his parents, Akell died in his sleep.

"He had always been a frail old man," Eleazar thought to himself. "It was as if he were staying alive just long enough to set me on the right path."

After burying Akell, Eleazar returned home. His parents were saddened by the news of Akell's death but were overjoyed to have their son home. And not only that, but to have him be courteous, kind, gentle and even loving toward all the members of his family. Akell had worked a miracle.

Even Eleazar's two best friends were impressed by the change. And because they had always tried to be like him for as far back as they could remember they did their best to copy his new attitude.

Fourteen months after Akell's death Eleazar went to his mother. "Mother, do you know what is going on? Father has taken on more jobs than we can do without hiring help. But from the way he speaks to others, I can tell that he has no intention of doing that. And several of the jobs are so small that he wouldn't have bothered with them a year ago. Do you know why he is doing all of this?"

"Did you ask your father?" she asked quietly.

"Yes, he said he was just making the business stronger. But that does not explain why he is working so much harder. He and his work have a good reputation and we are making more money than ever before."

His mother said a quick prayer under her breath, asking for forgiveness then said, "do you remember the client who died before the work had even started?"

"Yes, Soret son of Matthew."

"Well, his house was to contain the finest marble. Your father had to borrow five thousand pieces of silver to buy the materials. But then a lion killed Soret while he was out hunting. His family decided not to build the new house.

That left your father with a lot of marble which none wanted and a large debt that he could not begin to pay off without a very big job or a large number of smaller ones. And to make things even worse, the Egyptian your father borrowed from has threatened to have your father work off the debt as a slave in Egypt if he cannot keep up with the payments. Eleazar, I don't know what to do. We cannot survive if your father is made a slave."

Eleazar was very concerned, but no matter how hard he tried he could not think of a way to make more money for his father, other than helping him with his work in the same way he had been doing for the past year. Three days after he had heard the real reason for his father's push to make more money, Eleazar overheard two men speaking while he was waiting his turn to present his sin offering.

"Over in Gibeion they are offering one thousand pieces of silver to anyone who will help stop the Philistine raids on their crops and livestock."

"That's a lot of money, for what, a week? It should not take longer than that to track the dogs down and put them to the sword."

A thousand pieces of silver for a week's work, that sounded great to Eleazar. If he hired himself out as a mercenary he would be able to pay off his father's debt in just a month or two and save his father from years of slavery.

He went to Gibeion; three days walk, and took Akell's sword with him. His father found his note four hours after he had left.

"I will be gone for a month, maybe less. I have found a way to make some extra money. I know that you are a proud man and will not ask for help, but you are my father and I would be a poor son if I simply stood by and watched as you were taken into slavery.

God be with us all,

Eleazar

When he reached Gibeion there was a camp of some thirty men just outside of town. Eleazar went there first; thinking that it seemed to be the place where fighting men would gather. He stopped a man on the outskirts of the camp. "Where can I find the man in charge of hiring the fighting men?

"That would be Steven, his tent is near the center of camp with two large dogs sitting just outside. Whatever you do, don't try to pet those dogs. They won't let anybody but Steven touch them.

Eleazar quickly found the tent and the two dogs. As he approached the tent the dogs never made a sound, they just watched as he scratched the tent's door.

"Who is it?" said a man's voice.

"Eleazar, son of Dodai. I've come to fight the Philistines."

"You've cut it pretty close my friend," said the voice from inside growing closer. "We will surely go out to meet our enemy..." He had pushed back the tent flap and stopped when he saw Eleazar.

"You're just a boy. A very large boy, but still a boy. Go home, and come back when you have a beard."

"I must have the money and I am good with the sword."

Steven looked Eleazar over from head to foot. "How many men have you killed, boy?"

"None."

"None? I thought you would have killed at least one, and then gotten full of yourself. I suppose the confidence to come here and earn a thousand pieces of silver not to mention surviving to spend it had to come from somewhere. So what is it? Did you have some sort of training?"

"Yes sir, a man named Akell taught me how to be a soldier. He was the former leader of the fighting men in
Ashon."

"Never heard of him." Steven reached inside the tent and brought out a sword. "Let's see what this Akell has taught you."

Eleazar's hand was already moving toward his sword. Which he had been wearing at his hip, when Steven who had his back to him, suddenly spun around and swung his sword at Eleazar's head. His intention was to give the boy a scar to remind him of how foolish he had been to try and become a mercenary. But Eleazar blocked the swing with his own sword and with such power as to send Steven spinning halfway around in the opposite direction and nearly knocking the sword from his grasp. Steven quickly regained his balance and turned his spinning motion into a swing from the other direction only to have something touch his chest just as he came around. He froze, with his sword still raised and ready to strike. He looked down to see the point of Eleazar's sword poised to pierce his heart. Steven stepped back and lowered his sword. Eleazar put his back in its sheath. There was applause and cheers from behind him. Eleazar turned and was surprised to find no less than a dozen men who had gathered to watch his encounter with Steven.

"Alright, the show's over," said Steven.

"Well," asked one of the men. "Are you going to let him fight?"

Steven looked at Eleazar with a newfound respect. "Yes, you stay close to me. The Philistines were seen yesterday. They will be here by morning. And we plan to ambush them."

The next morning Eleazar was more than a little nervous. To take his mind off of the coming battle, Steven explained the battle plan as they walked to the ambush site in the predawn darkness.

"The Philistines fight best when they form columns and rows, called a phalanx. That way they can hide behind their big shields and stab at you with their spears. What we're going to do is destroy their order and not give them a chance to recover. The fact that Gibeion sits on top of a mountain works to our advantage. The road the Philistines are marching on passes through a narrow valley, at the end of which, is a hill that the road climbs. Ten of our men will hide on the right side of the road, and ten will hide on the left. After the Philistines pass by, the remaining ten will come, screaming, down the road with the rising sun at their backs. Not knowing how many are attacking them, the

Philistines will want to retreat a safe distance and form the phalanx, but the two hidden groups will attack from the sides before they have a chance to do so. That is how thirty will defeat a hundred."

The plan was executed just the way Steven had described it. Eleazar was with him on the right hand side of the road when they ran out to meet the retreating band of raiders. Eleazar encountered a soldier who had lost his shield. But he still had his spear. Eleazar dodged the thrust at his head and struck the man a powerful slashing blow that sent him nearly flying backward. Eleazar looked down at the fallen mans face; it was split open from forehead to chin.

"Hey!" yelled Steven. "Don't look at the bodies. Find your next man. Get the job done."

Eleazar nodded and quickly found his next man and then another, and then it was over. All of the Philistines were dead and only two mercenaries had been killed.

The next seven days the men stayed in camp until the towns priest said that they were no longer unclean from the touching of dead bodies. The people of Gibeion paid them their silver and held a feast in their honor. At the feast Steven asked Eleazar a question.

"So, what do you plan to do with all of that silver?"

"My father is in debt and will be made a slave if he does not keep up his payments. He needs another four thousand silver pieces in addition to what I have now."

"I see. Eleazar, you did very well in battle. I believe you can earn the money for your father and much more. But you should know that most people who are looking for mercenaries do not wish to hire them one at a time but would rather hire a company of men such as we have here. Join us, and you will find it much easier to gain employment as a mercenary."

Eleazar thought about it for a moment and found no fault in Steven's reasoning. He extended his hand. "Thank you Steven, I will gladly add my sword to your number."

Eleazar fought in three more campaigns. At the end of each adventure he took time to journey home and make payment on his fathers debt until it was paid in full.

"What's it like Eleazar, to travel all over and see the world?"

"My friends, do not be jealous of me. It is not an easy life I have chosen. Being paid to fight, is very dangerous. I have come close to death many times, yet I still live and have suffered no permanent injuries. I believe this is so because of the advice my father gave me when I was a boy. It's hard to believe that it was only five years ago. My father told me to pray for the Lord's protection every day, and if I kept myself righteous and repented for my sins the Lord would grant my request and keep me safe."

"Yea, we know about that Eleazar," said Hagri. "But we also know you like hacking the enemy to pieces. How many men have you killed?"

"Don't be foolish," said Ira. "He doesn't have time for counting the dead, he would be would be to busy trying not to become one of them. Isn't that right, Eleazar?"

"Yes, you are right. But Hagri is right also. I do love a good fight."

"Hey that reminds me." Said Hagri; "do you remember that guy who lived on the south side of the olive grove. His father was a saddle maker."

"He made more than just saddles, but yes I remember him, Paul, son of Etimus. He was the only guy I ever fought who made me afraid that I might loose."

"Would have severed you right if you had." Ira laughed, "Picking a fight with the one boy in town who was bigger and stronger than you."

Eleazar grinned. "Well its like I said. I do love a good fight."

"If you ask me, I'd say you're a crazy man. That was the longest fight I ever saw. You two were pounding on each other for almost an hour. And the only reason you won was because he passed out two heart beats before you did."

Eleazar laughed along with his two friends even though he winced, just a little when he remembered how his entire body hurt after he woke up.

"You know," said Hagri, "he married Tirna last month."

"He did?!" said Eleazar, shocked. "Yeah, the prettiest girl in town." Said Ira.

"The one who was so beautiful that we crawled through the reeds down by the stream so that we could watch her bathe." Sighed Eleazar.

"I still think she knew we were there." Said Hagri. "We made enough noise crawling through those reeds to wake the dead."

"Well, if she did know someone was watching her she certainly didn't seem to mind." Said Ira. "Speaking of beautiful girls, isn't that your sister coming out of the weavers shop, Eleazar?"

"Yes, that's Tamuz."

"She's old enough to get married now that her birthday has passed." Said Hagri, "Has your father decided on a husband for her yet?"

"Why," asked Eleazar, "are you looking for a second wife?"

"Far be it from me to take a second wife before my two best friends have found even one. People would say I was greedy."

"Go ahead, be greedy." Said Ira. "I'm not taking a wife until I build my house and I don't plan to start on it until next year."

"I wouldn't do it anyway. Tamuz is like a sister to me, and I like a brother to her. I doubt either of us would be very comfortable…"

Eleazar interrupted, "Who is that fellow talking to Tamuz?"

""That's Zuari. His family settled here shortly after you left for your last job. His father is a very skilled potter." Said Ira.

As the three friends watched from the concealing shadows of the shade tree they were seated under, Zuari reached out and grasped Tamuz's breast and began to caress it. She was so shocked at the sudden violation that Tamuz just stood there for a moment as if frozen. Then quickly pushed his hand away and ran toward home. Zuari laughed as he watched her go.

A dark seething anger welled up in Eleazar. "Did you see that?" asked Ira.

"Yes, I saw," said Hagri.

Ira turned to look at his friend as Eleazar got up and started walking in the opposite direction. "Aren't you going to say anything to him, Eleazar?" He and Hagri quickly got up and followed Eleazar's quick and purposeful steps.

"Yes, I will speak with him," said Eleazar, "but first I'm going to get my sword."

There was no one in the house when Eleazar and his friends arrived. "Where is everyone?" asked Hagri.

"Mother's been looking for good pasturage to buy. The herd is starting to get too big for what we have. Tamuz probably went to find her and took the cook with her since the hired man is likely with my mother."

After retrieving his sword, Eleazar and Hagri followed Ira to Zuari's house. It was nearly time for the midday meal so that seemed like the best place to find him. When they arrived Eleazar knocked on the door. "Come in," said a man's voice.

It was he, Zuari. Dipping bread into a steaming bowl of soup. He must have started it cooking before he left that morning.

"I am Eleazar son of Dodai. The girl Tamuz is my sister. Do you intend to ask my father for her in marriage?"

"What, is this a joke?" asked Zuari disbelievingly.

"We saw you in front of the weaver's shop." Said Eleazar.

Zuari's eyes narrowed and he looked at the three men shrewdly.

"You touched my sister in a way that only a husband should touch his wife, and then only in their bed chamber, not on a public street as if you were deciding whether or not to buy the services of a prostitute."

"I was simply having a little fun. Your sister was not harmed and no, I have no intention of making a girl like her my wife." Zuari said snidely.

"What do you mean, a girl like her?" asked Eleazar, his hand moving closer to his sword. Zuari did not notice the motion but Hagri and Ira did. They prepared themselves for action.

"I mean, none of the little harlots in this town are good enough for me. I'll get a wife from Samaria. City girls are more interesting. Now get out of my house." He said with a flippant wave of his hand, as if dismissing irritating servants.

"That's enough," said Eleazar as he drew his sword. "Grab him!"

Zuari jumped out of his chair, upsetting the bowl of soup when he bumped the table as Hagri and Ira reached for him. They threw him across the table but he was too strong, they couldn't hold him still. Zuari was about to break free when Eleazar took a brass pot from a nearby shelf and hit him in the head with it. Zuari was unconscious.

"Put him in position." Commanded Eleazar.

They did so quickly. And Eleazar lifted his sword. Zuari awoke and opened his eyes just in time to see the sword come down and pass through his wrist. Zuari made a screaming face but no sound came from his mouth. Hagri quickly brought out the thick cloth that he had brought along just in case the situation went as far as it had, and pressed it against the stump of Zuari's right wrist. Once the initial pain had subsided Zuari could speak.

"Please, do not leave me like this. Everyone will think I am a thief. I will not be able to work, no one will buy from me, no man would give me his daughter as a wife."

"No one will think you a thief. We will make your crime known to everyone." Said Eleazar.

"No," screamed Zuari. "They would take me out and stone me. Be merciful, kill me now. Kill me with your sword." Hagri and Ira looked at Zuari kneeling on the floor, and then at Eleazar. He stood there for a moment, thinking.

Then said, "very well, I will do as you ask."

Zuari threw open his arms to receive the thrust, and Eleazar pierced his heart.

"Lay him on his back and cover him, in case his mother comes by before his father can be told what has happened."

They left Zuari's house and went straight to the place where Dodai, Eleazar's father was cutting stone for a rich customer's new patio. They told him everything that had happened.

"You have done only what the law demands. You have two witnesses who will testify on your behalf. You have done nothing wrong. And yet, it would be best for you and our whole family if you left town."

"Why?" asked Eleazar. "You just said I did only what the law demands."

"Yes, I did. But Zuari's father is a man of short temper and unforgiving spirit. He will need time to calm down, to even begin to believe what three young men have to say about his son. Even if it is completely believable to everyone else."

Eleazar closed his eyes and sighed heavily. "Alright father I will leave before sunrise."

"My son, I know that you are good at being a soldier. But what you have been doing is too dangerous. Hear your father, be a soldier, but not one who fights constantly to keep money in his purse. The king's soldier's fight less often and are paid regularly. Become one of them, so that your mother and I will not constantly wonder, is this the day our son will die?"

"I never realized you worried about me so much."

"You are our son, how could we not?"

Eleazar crossed the room and hugged his father, they both had tears in their eyes. "Yes, father," said Eleazar. "I will join the king's army."

Less than three months later Eleazar was with King David when he took control of Jerusalem.

Some time later David led his thirty-seven Mighty Men into battle against the Philistines gathered at Pas Dammim. The plan was to merely harass them and quickly retreat in order to determine their numbers.. All went according to plan, but during the retreat as they were crossing a field of barley, Eleazar, son of Dodai the Ahohite, heard the voice of God.

"Turn back, and face your enemy, and I will deliver them into your hand."

Now Eleazar was in the back of the group. So no one saw him stop his horse in the middle of the barley field and turn back to face the much larger group of Philistines that was chasing them. He got off his horse and drew his sword and attacked his enemies.

At the appointed place in the nearby hills the Mighty Men counted their number and realized that Eleazar was not among them.

"He should be here," said Eliam. "He was behind me when I entered the barley field."

"I'll go back," said Adino. "He could be lying in that field with an arrow in his back."

"No," said David. "We will all go."

They approached the barley field cautiously, wary of any hidden Philistines. But all they found in the field was

Eleazar, sitting amongst hundreds of dead men.

Eleazar looked up at his friend Adino as he quickly dismounted and ran to his side. "Are you hurt?" asked Adino.

"I could use some help with my sword. My hand seems to be frozen to it." Eleazar gave a tired laugh. David, who was nearby looked about himself and said, "The Lord has brought about a great victory today. There is nothing left for us to do except to strip the dead."

Adino

"Husband, is it safe to give him such a toy?"

"Of course it's safe. He's seven years old, and I've spoken to him many times about how weapons should be handled."

"Well, if you say so. But, did you have to make it look so real?"

"It's just a staff, painted to look like a spear."

While his parents discussed his new toy Adino was outside pretending to be a great warrior. He had been playing for only a few minutes when Jakin, Ozni and Tola came walking down the street.

Adino's family lived on the edge of town next to his father's shop. He was a skilled weapons maker and men came from all over to buy his father's weapons or to hire him to make something special.

"Well, what do we have here?" said Jakin. He was the oldest, eleven; Ozni and Tola were ten. "It looks like a toy spear," said Tola.

"Let me hold it for a minute," said Jakin, holding out his hand.

Adino had seen these three in action before. They liked to take smaller children's toys and not give them back until they were broken. He didn't like them, not even a little and he had no intention of just handing over his spear.

"No, it's mine, and you can't have it." Said Adino as he shifted to a ready position.

"Don't be stupid," said Jakin. "If you make me take it from you you're going to get hurt, owe!"

Adino had taken a step forward and thrust the spear at Jakin's mouth. The older boy dropped to his knees and doubled over with pain as he held his bruised and bleeding lips.

Instinctively taking advantage of the other two boys surprise, Adino used Jakin's back as a platform and sprang into the air using his spear like a quarter staff, he slapped the butt end into Tola's eye and then smacked the blunt tip into Ozni's nose. He landed behind them with a bit of a stumble then turned around and resumed his ready position. But the three older boys wanted nothing else to do with him.

"He hit me in the eye!!" yelled Tola, holding his eye with tears streaming out from under his hand. Ozni was to busy trying to see where he was walking while tilting his head back and pinching his bleeding nose, to comment. But Jakin turned back, and through quickly swelling lips said, "You're going to pay for this."

But, after their parents learned that they received their wounds while trying to steal a small boy's toy, the three bullies spent so much time in the fields plowing, planting, weeding and watering that they were to tired to get revenge.

Adino spent the next four years living what he remembered as the best years of his life. He spent most of his time just watching. He watched his father, a master at making weapons of every sort. He watched his mother as she danced. She loved to dance. She knew many different dances, all of which were taught to her by her grandmother, who had grown up in Central Asia.

One day while he was helping his father make a sword for his uncle Gahar, Adino heard screaming. Not just from women but men as well, coming from the far side of town. His father must have heard it as well. He suddenly dropped the sword in the cooling trough, before it was time to do so, and snatched a finished sword from it's hanging place on the wall.

"We're under attack," he said to Adino. "Where is your mother and sisters?"

"She went to the well for water. The girls are playing in front of the house." He answered quickly. "Take your sisters and hide in the refuse pit."

"Yes father."

Adino realized that he must have questioned his father with his eyes, and that his father must be very worried because he took time to explain.

"I know it's disgusting and that you will make yourselves unclean. But because of the stench no one will look for you there. If your sisters protest, throw them in and stay quiet. Do not come out until I come for you."

"Yes, father," said Adino. Then he ran to find his two little sisters.

The refuse pit was dug into the side of a hill, overlooking Adino's home. One side of the pit was sloped. This allowed the children to lie there without being seen, unless someone walked right up to the edge, without having to touch the pit's contents. There was tall grass near the pit so Adino could crawl forward a little and look down on the house. What he saw burned into his memory and helped shape the rest of his life.

Two men were with his father; they were all standing with their backs to one another. Adino was to far away to make out their faces. But five Philistines surrounded them. One of the men with his father fell quickly and then the other. His father fought on for a few seconds longer, but five opponents were more than he could handle. First one sword and then another found it's mark, and he was soon lying on the ground motionless, like the others. His father was dead. As the tears started to form in his eyes Adino heard a woman scream off to his right. It was his mother. The water jar lay on the ground broken where she had dropped it. She was running as fast as she could to her fallen husband as if the Philistine soldiers weren't even there. But she never reached him. One of the soldiers grabbed her and tried to force himself upon her. She kneed him in the groin, so desperate to get to her husband that she didn't think but simply reacted. Such a blow would earn her a quick death among her own people. The Philistines also had this law. While their comrade was still rolling on the ground with his hands between his legs the other Philistines drew their swords as one and struck down Adino's mother.

But Adino did not see them kill and then literally hack his mother to pieces. He had looked away, not able to bear the sight of his mother being killed. He crawled back to the refuse pit and did his best to keep his sisters from crying to loudly. Though they saw nothing they heard and could tell by the tears on Adino's face what must have happened. The three of them huddled together and cried themselves to sleep.

They awoke the next morning to the sound of a familiar voice calling their names. It was their father's brother Uncle Gahar.

"It's Uncle Gahar," said the girls simultaneously.

"Quiet," whispered Adino. "I'll see if it's safe first." He already knew that if uncle Gahar was calling out to them it must be safe. But he wanted to try and keep the girls from seeing their dead parents. The moment he peeked through the brush he realized that he should not have worried at all. The men with his uncle were carrying away a large blanket, which he assumed held the pieces of his mother. His father's body was already gone, as were the bodies of the two men who had fought at his father's side.

Adino told his sisters to come out, then stood and waved so that his uncle could see him. After he and his sisters had washed the smell of the refuse pit off of them and had a large meal, uncle Gahar took Adino to his father's shop. The walls were lined with weapons of every size and shape one could imagine. Adino could name them all. He had watched his father make most of them.

"All of these belong to you now. If you like I will have my men find buyers for them and in that way you can provide dowries for your sisters." Said Gahar.

"But we will need money for food and clothes and I do not have my father's talent for making weapons." Lamented Adino.

"You are my brother's children, since he is gone you are now my children. I will feed and clothe you." He looked around the room at the many weapons that surrounded them. "Would you like to keep some of these, to remember your father by?"

Adino looked around the room then said to Gahar, "Uncle, if it's alright with you, I would like to honor my father by learning to use every type of weapon he made."

"Are you sure you wish to do that? There are so many."

"Yes, I will take one of each kind, especially this." He walked over to a cabinet, opened it and removed something wrapped in a large cloth. Adino removed the wrapping to reveal a spear.

"Father tried to hide it from me but I heard him tell mother about it. He was waiting to give it to me when I become a man. The head is made for slashing as well as stabbing, the shaft is as supple as it is strong, and the metal ball on the end helps to balance it and makes a good club. He said it was the finest spear he had ever made." Adino looked up at his uncle with tears in his eyes.

"Come, let us set it and the other weapons aside so that my men do not sell them by mistake."

"Master Gahar, Master Gahar, the caravan from Samaria has been attacked by a band of thieves," Said a servant as he ran up to the house.

Gahar dropped his cup, spilling wine across the table. "What of my son?" he asked with a shaken tone. "He and two others survived, though they were all badly wounded. The guardsmen is not expected to live through the night."

"Where are they?"

"The home of Phinnius, the potter. I will send men and have them brought here at once."

"No, let them stay where they are. See to it that Moleb cares for them, he is the best physician. Give Phinnius a silver coin for every day they are there and five gold coins on the day they leave. And see to it that my horse is made ready. I will go up to them immediately. Send Adino after me as soon as he returns.

Ever since the murder of their parents by the Philistines, Adino and his two sisters had lived with their uncle Gahar.

Gahar was a wealthy merchant, who traded with many people in many different lands. Even as far away as Asia, which was where Adino's mother was from.

They had been living with him in Ramoth Gilead for seven years and were treated like his own four daughters and one son. Michael was the oldest at twenty-one. Adino had learned much about the merchant trade from his uncle, but had learned more from his cousin Michael, and loved him like a brother. When he heard that Michael had been wounded he grabbed his spear, which was never far from him, and nearly killed one of his uncles best horses by forcing it to sprint all the way to the potters secluded home. His uncle and Phinnius were standing outside talking when he arrived.

"How is Michael doing, Uncle?"

"He will live, but the physician says that his sword arm will never be as strong as it was."

"Praise God. Was he able to tell you about the bandits? Where they might be from or where they went?"

"First, let me introduce you to our host, Phinnius."

"My apologies," Adino said to the potter. "I was so concerned for my cousin that I have forgotten my manners."

"I understand," said Phinnius. "Please, come in and speak with your cousin while I have my wife prepare you some food."

Adino and his uncle went in to speak with Michael. His right arm was heavily bandaged and he was pale. But he sounded just a little tired, when he spoke and appeared to be in good spirits.

"No, I was unconscious, so I did not see which direction they left in but they were traveling with a group of Philistine soldiers."

"What!" shouted Adino and Gahar together.

"Yes, it appears that the Philistines have found yet another way in which to plague us."

The three of them sat for a moment letting the news sink in, Michael with his head back and his eyes closed.

Trying not to let on to the others that his arm was aching, Adino glaring at the floor with a fresh and consuming hatred of the Philistines. And Gahar thoughtfully stroking his beard.

"As much as I hate to do this I can see no other way," said Gahar. "Adino, I want you to lead the caravan to Dan."

"But father, he is not ready. He has had no training in dealing with customers or haggling…"

"Never the less, I am sending him. The loss of this last caravan was very costly. The one I am taking south to Ziklag will not cover my debts. I must have two caravans, two successful caravans in order to pay off the debts and have enough left over to live on and to continue as a merchant."

"When must I leave, uncle?" asked Adino, trying to sound ready for anything. But his uncle and cousin knew that he was nervous about leading a caravan on his own for the first time. "In two days. And I will send Molatt with you."

"Your old house slave? Why send him along?"

"He is not a slave, but I understand how you might make that mistake. I freed him many years ago, but he loved me like a brother and could not bear the thought of leaving. He knows my trade almost as well as I. He will make an excellent adviser. Be sure to have him with you when ever you are doing business."

"And if we are attacked?"

"I can only pray that such will not be the case."

Four days later Adino was riding his camel through the hilly and rocky lands just south of Hazor. The sun was getting low. It would soon be time to make camp for the evening.

Adino turned sideways on his mount so that he could look back and see the caravan drawn out behind him.

Forty camels, all loaded with herbs, spices, cloths, scented oils, tapestries and dozens of other goods. It was worth a small fortune, and he was responsible for it all. He shook his head.

"I must not think about it, it will only make me nervous." He said to himself.

As he watched the heavily loaded camels striding along in his wake his attention was suddenly drawn to a large stand of brush, off to his right. A swarm of sticks had risen from it and were arching across the sky towards the caravan's guards.

"We are under attack," yelled Adino. But it was too late. The arrows fell among the guards. Two men and a horse went down.

Adino quickly returned to a forward position when he heard the sound of several horses running. Descending the hill before him, with the sun at their backs, were a hundred men. Adino kicked his camel to a run and headed for the brush were the archers were hidden. A second volley of arrows had just found their marks and a quick glance revealed that one more man was on the ground and several others were wounded.

As he drew near their position, the archers, there were five of them, took aim and fired at his camel. The beast collapsed beneath him with arrows in its neck and breast. Adino freed his spear from its straps and leapt clear of the falling animal. He rolled twice then sprang to his feet running toward the archers with his spear at the ready. They calmly took their time and knocked another arrow. All five of them took aim at the easy target sprinting toward them. Almost as one they released, sending certain death toward Adino's chest. But with amazing quickness and agility Adino swatted all five arrows away like insects. The archers just stood there gaping at him in astonishment. By the time the first one realized that they were in danger it was too late. Adino was among them and three seconds later all five archers were dead or dying.

He saw the archers' horses, tied to a near by thicket. He took one and rode as fast as he could back to the caravan. As he rode he saw that things were not going well for the guardsmen. At full strength they would have been out numbered two to one. But with several injured or killed by the archers, it was even worse.

He watched as the bandits fell upon the guardsmen. Adino kicked the horse frantically, trying to get even more speed out of the animal and as he rode he said this prayer. "Lord, God of Israel, help me to save my brothers." A few moments later he entered the fray and used his spear with such speed and accuracy that to the guardsmen who saw him he appeared to merely ride through the chaos and the enemy dropped dead at his passing. But one of them managed to stick a spear into Adino's horse, piercing its heart. It dropped dead instantly, throwing Adino headfirst through the air. Acting purely on instinct he tucked his head and rolled into a ball. He hit the ground hard enough to bruise his shoulders but to his surprise there was no other damage. He had no idea where his spear was; he had dropped it when he hit the ground. He found himself lying next to a fallen bandit, who had on his belt a bladed whip.

The blade was not large, just a little bigger than an arrowhead, but it was very sharp. The hours of practice he had spent with the one from his fathers shop flooded his mind as he snatched the weapon from its resting-place and got to his feet. Three bandits ran toward him with their swords lifted high.

Adino rolled out the whip behind him and made a low snap at the first bandit, slashing his right knee deeply. Without hesitating he aimed the next stroke at the second man and slashed his throat.

The third bandit stopped himself as quickly as he could, trying to stay out of range of the whip. But Adino took two steps toward him and cracked his whip once again. The stroke left a deep cut in the bandit's forearm causing his sword to fly off to the side.

Adino dropped the whip and ran for the sword. The man with the gashed knee tried to beat him to it but he couldn't make his injured leg move fast enough. He reached the sword only a moment after Adino. But instead of reaching down to pickup the weapon, it came up to meet him, clasped firmly in Adino's hand. It plunged deep into his stomach and was snatched free as Adino ran past him to the bandit with the injured arm.

Seeing that Adino meant to end his life, the bandit searched the ground frantically for a weapon. He saw and quickly picked up a spear.

It was so close that he was surprised that he hadn't stepped on it. As Adino ran toward him these thoughts flashed through his mind.

"This is a good spear, well balanced and…" He didn't get to complete the thought. Adino had fainted left then shifted right, allowing a clumsy spear thrust to pass over his left shoulder, and pushed his sword between his opponents ribs, just below the left arm pit. As the bandit started to fall away, Adino let go of the sword, leaving it in the mans side and with his left hand, snatched his spear from the falling mans hands.

Adino looked down at the weapon his father had made for him, and took a moment, just a brief pause, to savor the feel of it in his hands. As he thought, "I missed you old friend, lets get to work."

"Then Adino danced into battle. I know it sounds ridicules, but it was no dance I had ever seen before. No, that's not true, I had seen it before and so have you. It was the same dance that he does when he says he is practicing with his spear. Except this time it wasn't just him and his spear. He danced into a crowd of bloodthirsty killers, killers, who were winning the battle. My men could have handled any of them one on one, but they were being attacked by groups of three or more. And with an arrow in my leg, even I was barley able to defend my self.

Then came Adino. "This isn't the practice field, you can die out here boy." That's what I thought, and in the time it took to form that thought he had killed two men. He was quick, precise, and deadly. The other bandits seemed to forget about the rest of us; they all focused on Adino and his deadly dance. At first they laughed at him but shortly the only sounds were the clash of weapons, the stamping of feet the screams of the wounded and the thump of the dead as they hit the ground. Three, perhaps four minutes was all it took. Though at the time it seemed much longer. Then I heard one of the bandits say to another. "We must flee, this one fights as if God himself were his teacher." The other agreed, and they sounded the retreat.

I could hardly believe it. My men and I were like dead dogs to these bandits, but they fled from Adino, and for good reason. I counted the bodies myself. At his feet lay no less than thirty men. Fifty-five bandits were killed that day, and I found out later that Adino also killed eighteen of the twenty-five additional dead men.

Gahar, your nephew is a warrior without equal."

"Thank you Captain Lemit, rest now, you've earned it." Gahar climbed wearily to his feet and made his exit, stopping briefly to remind Lemit's wife to contact him if they should need anything.

Still dusty from his own, uneventful business trip, Gahar mounted his camel and headed for home. He hardly noticed how long it took. His mind kept replaying the tales he had heard of Adino's great battle. First from his old friend Molatt, who had wisely stayed well away from the battle, but he had heard Adino's shout, that they were being attacked. And he saw the quick work; Adino made of the archers. The guardsmen told him how Adino rode into battle, leaving all with the impression that the bandits dropped dead simply because he crossed their path. Now, Captain Lemit's account. It all seemed so unbelievable and yet, here were all of these witnesses. It had been surprise enough to have a messenger meet him just as his own returning caravan came in sight of the city.

"Gahar," yelled the messenger. It was one of his servants. Gahar waved him over. "Adino's caravan was attacked!"

"God be merciful," said Gahar. "What of my nephew? What of Adino?"

"He is not harmed, sir. I also have a message for you from Adino. He says that nothing was lost, and though they arrived three days late all business was completed. Also, several of the customers aided in caring for the wounded. Twenty-five of the bandit's horses were captured and sold. He asked Captain Lemit to divide the money from the bandit horses among the widows of the guardsmen who were killed in addition to the pay they were to receive."

"Very good, I agree completely." Said Gahar. "Take this message back to my nephew.

I will visit Molatt and Lemit before turning home. Have a feast prepared to celebrate our success."

Gahar arrived home to the sound of musicians and laughter. Adino meet him at the gate. "You are late for your own party." Said Adino Gahar just laughed as he dismounted and gave his nephew a big hug.

The next morning Adino went to his uncle, who was having a late breakfast.

"Uncle, I need to talk with you about something very important to me."

"I know what you're going to say Adino. It was obvious at the party last night. You have decided that all of your training has paid off and that you are now ready to go out and help rid our land of the Philistines once and for all. I know that you have been saving your money so as to build up dowries for your sisters. Even though I wished other wise I suppose I've always known that this day would eventually come. I believe you could have been a fine merchant, but the reports I got from Molatt and Lemit tell me that you will make a far better warrior."

"Then I have your blessing?" Adino asked smiling broadly.

"Yes, go, and make the Philistines regret ever setting foot in Israel."

"Adino, I was watching you during the battle today. Who taught you to fight like that?" asked Poean the Egyptian.

"It is my own fighting style. I invented it to honor my mother." Said Adino.

They were sitting with the other mercenaries, having their evening meal. They had all been hired by the people of Kadesh Barnea to stop the Philistine raids on their fields.

"Then, your mother is dead?" Poean asked.

"Yes, she and my father were killed by the Philistines when I was eleven. My mother loved to dance; so in order to honor her I used several of her dances in the creation of my fighting style. I believe that God approves of the way in which I honored my mother and has helped me to be successful in the creation of an effective fighting style."

"But, what of your father? How did you honor him?" Poean asked.

"My father was a skilled craftsman. He made several different types of weapons. To honor him, I learned how to use every weapon he made. Though you may have noticed that the spear is my favorite."

Poean nodded his approval, then said. "I have also noticed that you have a certain hatred for the Philistines. Now I understand why. But you are an Israelite, aren't you?'

Adino looked at him suspiciously and took note of the position of Poean's sheaved sword. "Yes." He said slowly. Some Egyptians did not care for Israelites.

Poean continued, "Well if you hate the Philistines and they do seem to be an unending source of trouble for your people, why don't you join the kings army and help get rid of them forever?"

"You know." said Adino, intrigued. "I never thought of that. King Saul does hate the Philistines."

"You know if you really want to impress him, I heard that theirs a traitorous general that he has half of his army searching the country side for. A fellow named David. If you found where he and his men were hiding and took that information to King Saul, who knows, he might make you a leader of hundreds."

Adino laughed. "I think I would rather be a simple soldier." But he gave the idea of finding General David much consideration.

A month later Adino found himself in Hebron. He had learned many things after he and his fellow mercenaries had run the Philistines out of Kadesh Barnea. The most important of which was that no one seemed to know why David was called a traitor. Also, when sent out to lead a search party, the king's own son showed little interest in finding the man. And when they heard that General David had gone into hiding hundreds of fighting men left their homes and went to join him.

Adino decided that before he did anything else he should find the real reason behind King Saul's desire to see his best and most famous general dead. He discovered that David and his men were hiding in Philistia. The very last place that King Saul would think to look for the slayer of the Philistines giant, Goliath. But on the morning that he was to start his journey to Philistia Adino over heard a conversation at breakfast between to merchants.

"Saul is dead you say?" asked the first merchant.

"Yes," said the second. "His body and that of three of his four sons, was hung on the wall at Beth Shan. But just a few days ago the brave men of my hometown, Jabesh Gilead, went and took down the bodies. They burned them, so that they could not be abused further and buried their bones in Jabesh."

"King Saul is dead?" Thought Adino, to himself. "That means that David should be returning to Israel. Unless Saul's surviving son wishes to see David dead, just as his father had."

Then the first merchant said. "So that leaves only Ish-Bosheth as Saul's only living son, he should be anointed king."

"Perhaps," said the second merchant. "But I have not heard good things about this Ish-Bosheth. It is said that he is a spoiled prince and of weak character. Which may explain why he was at home while his father and brothers were fighting and dying for Israel. A better choice would be one of Saul's commanders. Like Abner, son of Ner. He would make a good king."

A very large young man seated at an adjacent table turned to the two merchants and said. "You should be careful how you speak of the Prince and future king of Israel. His friends might hear you and decide it necessary to beat some respect into you."

He was smiling when he said this, so the merchants were not sure if he were warning or merely joking with them. But with a man of his size it seemed best not to take any chances. They both apologized for their negative statements and quickly paid for their meals then left.

The large man chuckled to himself as they left.

Adino got up from his table and asked him, "Why did you frighten those men like that? You weren't insulted by what they said."

"True," said the big man. "But perhaps this experience will keep them from harm after Ish-Bosheth is anointed king. Weak men with power can be cruel to those who speak of their weakness openly."

"Then you frightened those men for nothing." Said a voice from behind them.

Adino and the large man turned and saw a group of men sharing a table in the corner. One of the men, a small but well muscled fellow got up and walked over to them.

"My name is Shammah son of Agee." Said the small man. "Eleazar son of Dodai." Said the large fellow.

"I am Adino, what do you mean he frightened them for nothing?"

"Well, I don't know why I feel a need to share this with two strangers but I have a strong feeling that I should." Shammah invited the others to sit at Eleazar's table and told them about his meeting with the prophet Samuel.

Over the next week the three men got to know each other better and quickly became the best of friends. When they finally got to meet David it was obvious to him that these three belonged together. So he had them housed in the same tent and later placed them under the same commander.

A few weeks later David's thirty-seven Mighty Men were camped in the mountains. The area if approached from the south could only be reached through a narrow twisting turning path that wound amongst the boulders.

Adino had been assigned guard duty with instructions to wake everyone if the Philistines should start up the path.

About three hours into his watch Adino heard noises further down the mountain. From his vantage point atop one of the boulders he could just make out a large number of Philistines starting up the path in the moonlight. They were approaching in a two-man column because the path was so narrow that only two could use their swords effectively in case of attack.

Adino turned to worn the others, but the Spirit of the Lord came upon him and spoke these words. "Raise your spear against them and none shall reach your camp."

He felt calm and inexplicably confident, so he jumped down from the boulder and ran down the path toward the Philistines. He surprised the first two and was able to kill them before they could even reach for their swords. The second pair managed to get their swords free but had no time to defend themselves. The third pair was ready for him but one of them tripped over a fallen comrade and paid for his clumsiness with his life. The other got over anxious and rushed in for the kill while Adino was killing his partner only to impale himself on the waiting spear. The battle continued long into the night with Adino slowly backing up the path so that the dead and dying would not be under foot. God touched the eyes of the General commanding the Philistine troops, so he did not see that the bodies he stepped over belonged to his own men. He urged his men forward with promises of riches and fame for killing the Jews. After a long, slow advance up the mountain path the general and his two aids came face to face with Adino.

Only then, did God remove the scales from the general's eyes. He suddenly realized, as his aids were dying, that he was standing before one man, not an army, and that this one man had destroyed his entire command. In the last bend of the mountain path before entering the Jews camp, the General died without even trying to defend himself because of the fear in his heart.

The next morning one of the men entered the path way to relive Adino, but ran back shouting that there were dead men on the path.

David and the others picked their way down the path, ready for anything and wondering what had happened to Adino. They found him at the entrance, sitting on a large rock and singing praises to the Lord.

"Adino, do you know that there are eight hundred dead men on the path," asked David, "why didn't you call out?"

"I did not need help, God was with me."

David, with the help of the mighty men eventually drove the Philistines from Israel. And Solomon, David's son was able to rule in peace.